POLARIS
GHOST

ERIC G. WILSON

Outpost19 | San Francisco
outpost19.com

Wilson, Eric G.
         Polaris Ghost/ Eric G. Wilson
         ISBN: 9781944853365 (pbk)

OUTPOST19

ORIGINAL
PROVOCATIVE
READING

SHORT-ISH
SERIES

Full list at
outpost19.com/shortish

Parts of this book have appeared, in somewhat altered form, in the following magazines: *apt, Café Irreal, The Collagist, Crack the Spine, decomP, The Doctor T.J. Eckleburg Review, Eclectica, The FANZINE, Hotel Amerika, The Notre Dame Review, The Portland Review, Posit, Prelude, Prick of the Spindle, Thrice Fiction,* and *The Vestal Review.* I would like to thank the editors of these publications for allowing me to reprint here.

For Kevin Calhoun

P O L A R I S
G H O S T

ERIC G. WILSON

EPIGRAPH

Clear nights, 200 A.D., between one and two, the Peratae, those who pass through, walk into the desert. They find Draco in the sky. This is the star-serpent coiled around the axis. This is the portal to cold heaven. The soul rises through the scales, cools in ice God doesn't know about. Back down, numb, the soul falls. It strikes the sand. The grains are now crystals. In their glass, there is nothing that is not seen.

— James Basire, who taught
William Blake engraving

BOOK I

The cat the child was secretly feeding—the parents would have forbidden it—was growing fatter. The child was glad, for when the cat first appeared at the forest's edge, it did not even look like a cat. It was a skeleton jerking in a dark gray sack. But after feasting on the table scraps the child slid under the porch, the beast resembled a cat again. It was silver-gray like the bark on the ash-tree it liked to rub against, and its eyes were green or yellow according to the light, and it was big, too big for a normal cat, more the size of a small person walking on all fours.

But then the cat's belly became round. Did it have a stone in its gut, the child wondered, or that ball in the grandmother's story?

The grandmother was gray, too, her skin, her hair. Before she got buried she told how a ghost had a ball the size of a head and this ball wasn't magic as you might think, only strange, making the ghost believe things.

The child was old enough to know this ball was not inside the cat's belly, nor a stone. The child was also old enough to know that if the parents were asked what was rounding this cat's gut, they would say babies.

But there were no kittens. The child could tell by the way the belly, when touched, pulsed. It was like one large heart thudding, thudding, not like little squirming creatures.

One day when the child touched the beating gut, the cat hissed and scratched.

Weeks later, five red lines still marked the child's left hand. When the parents asked about these marks, the child said, I tripped on the rocks. The parents paused, but they never asked about the wound again. The pain kept the child awake nights.

One evening, when the child as usual placed the scraps under the porch, the cat did not appear. The child thought the cat might be deeper under the porch and so crawled under the porch all the way to the middle of the house. The cat was not there.

Through the boards in the floor of the house, the child heard the parents calling. The child waited. The lights went out and the parents walked upstairs and shut their door.

Most nights after the parents closed down, the child sat by the edge of the porch and looked at the cat's eyes, not green now but yellow in the fading light, and asked, "What do you do when you are all alone?"

The cat fell asleep.

The child imagined the cat was dreaming an answer to the question, though: "When I am alone, I do not feel alone because in the forest nothing is separate from anything else, everything hides in the same darkness."

Now the cat was gone. Did it leave what was in its gut behind? The child again searched under the porch. Nothing.

The child crawled from under the porch. There was no moon, but the bark on the ash-tree at the edge of the woods shined.

This was the cat's favorite tree, the tree the cat liked to rub against.

The cat was inside the tree.

So the child believed.

The child ran toward the tree but tripped on the head-sized rock between the house and the tree. The ground scraped the left hand. Blood appeared where the five stripes were. The hand ached anew.

The child limped to the tree. The wind was cold, even though it was summer. The child touched the bark. It did not pulse, thud, thud, as the cat's belly had done.

A sound other than the wind came from the other side of the tree and the child stepped toward the sound.

It was only the wind after all.

But the child was now in the forest. Since the parents had forbidden the forest, this was the first time.

The child stepped three more times into the forest and listened again for the sound that was not the wind.

There it was. A hissing. A cat's hissing.

The silver-gray cat was inside the forest.

The child had heard the gray cat hiss the day it scratched the hand. The child had also heard it hiss the day the parents had tried to coax the cat from under the porch. They had said it was bad luck for a creature like that to live under the house. They stuck their hands under the house and called, "Kitty, kitty." The cat hissed, and the parents returned to the house, shaking their heads. They spoke no more of the matter.

The cat was now hissing from inside the forest. The cat was in danger. The child would save the cat.

The child walked toward the sound, deeper into the forest.

The wind died down.

The child listened for the hissing.

Nothing.

The child called the cat.

"Kitty, kitty."

Nothing.

"Kitty."

Still nothing.

The child sat down.

The wind flared, it was cold.

The child wanted to look for the cat more but the pain in the hand pulsed and the darkness came alive and there was fear.

Where am I? Why did they let this happen?

That sick quivering in the belly was there, like the time the parents had accidentally locked the child in the cellar. For a day, maybe two, maybe three—the parents never said how long—the child was trapped. No one heard the calling. Only when the grandmother came down for potatoes was the child discovered.

The child now remembered the grandmother's story about the ghost.

The child stood up and ran but could not see and slammed into a tree and fell and was lying face upward and breathing hard.

Two eyes, bright as fire, head-sized, yellow-green-gray, hissing from the sky, only eyes, straight for the child's face.

The child screamed and rolled over.

But this was nothing terrible.

The child stood up, no longer afraid, and not lost, and walked to the house and entered, and fell asleep in the bed.

The child awoke. The sun was bright. The left hand,

covered in blood, ached.

Something was under the bed.

The child crawled out of bed and looked into the space between the floor and the bed.

The silver-gray skin rested on the floor like an empty sack. Blood stained the edges.

The child had not imagined two things had been inside all this time. Perhaps the smaller one had been inside the bigger, like the Russian dolls the grandmother had once given.

The heads really were not as round as the child had imagined, either. And the child should have known they would not be the heads of cats.

Nothing would now be forbidden. The child could feed the two bodies under the porch whenever he liked. He could walk into the forest. And he would no longer be lonely, since he was hiding in the same darkness as all the other creatures.

BOOK II

All the boy wanted to do was play. He had asked his mother that morning, a very bright morning, if he could play ball in his front yard. He would be very good, he said. He would promise not to kick the ball into the road.

His mother told him no, he could not play in the front yard on that day. It wouldn't look right, she said, since last night the boy across the street, a boy not much older than her boy, was killed in an accident. Think what terrible things the boy's parents might do, she added, if they saw a living boy play while their boy is dead.

The boy said he would not play hard. He said he would just stand under the tree and toss his ball up in the air and catch it and then toss it up again. His mother said no, the dead boy's parents shouldn't see another boy at all. Her boy must stay indoors.

The boy walked into a room and lay on the floor. He tossed his ball toward the ceiling. He imagined it hung in the air like magic, before falling back into his hands.

Then he rested the ball on his chest. It rose and fell with his breathing. He began to breathe hard. The ball rolled off his chest, onto the floor, and into the corner.

The boy was upset. The day was bright, and he really wanted to play. Why should he not? He barely knew the older boy across the street, just as his parents barely knew the dead boy's parents.

He tried to imagine what was happening inside the house across the street. Was the older boy in the house? If so, was he in a coffin? And what were the parents doing? Were they standing over their dead boy crying, or were they sitting in the kitchen drinking coffee and looking sad?

The boy also wondered how the older boy looked. Was he the same, or something terrible?

One night a long time ago the younger boy had sneaked out of bed after his parents had gone to sleep.

The boy had seen his father enter the house just before dinner, as he always did, but this time his father did not pause in the kitchen to ask about everybody's day. He had hurried into the room where he spent most of his weekends, a room he called his library, filled with books and black-and-white photographs of skies, waterfalls, and ice. The boy had noticed his father was carrying something black under his arm. It might have been a box. What was in it?

The boy's parents went to bed. The boy crept into the library and he turned on the lamp. He searched the room. He could not find the box anywhere. It was not on his father's desk or in the desk drawers. It was not on the book shelves. It was not under the couch where his father rested and sometimes slept the whole night.

The boy grew tired. He lay down on the couch. He looked at the ceiling. The lamp cast shadows there, and the boy imagined the shadows were alive. He noticed something in the ceiling that he had never noticed before. It was a door. It was a door to an attic. The boy did not know his house had an attic.

The boy put a chair under the door into the attic. Standing

on the chair, he could almost reach the small white rope hanging from the attic door. He stacked several thick books on the chair. He stood on the books. He reached the rope, and he pulled on the rope. The door opened. A folded ladder was attached to the inside of the door. The boy unfolded the ladder. It reached to the floor. The boy came down from the stack of books on the chair and climbed into the attic.

Though he could not see very well, the boy knew he had found the black box. There it was, lying alone on a dusty floor made of rough boards. The boy grabbed the box, no, it was a book. He hurried to the lamp.

The book was three inches thick. The cover was black. It smelled like the horse the boy had ridden last summer.

The boy opened the book. The first page was printed in another language, but hand-written under the title, in black ink, were words the boy understood: "To Otto, with love and yearning." The rest of the book was also in the strange language. Throughout were black-and-white photographs. The photographs showed extremely thin men and woman. They were naked. They looked like skeletons tightly wrapped in dull white plastic. They were all lying down, some side by side in a long row, others in a large pile. Most of them had their eyes closed, but the eyes of some were wide open, like they'd seen a ghost. Standing among these bodies were men in black suits and top hats. They were not looking at the bodies. They were looking at the sky or at each other. Far behind them was a tree.

The boy closed the book. He returned it to the attic, shut the attic door, killed the lamp, hurried back to bed. He could not sleep. He lay on his back and breathed hard.

Now, a long time later, the boy lay on his back again,

breathing hard, his ball in the corner. Did the older boy who had died in the accident look like the men and women in his father's black book?

The boy no longer cared about playing ball outside on this bright day. He wanted to see the older dead boy.

The boy called his mother. She appeared. He asked if she and his father were going to visit the family across the street. The mother said no. The boy asked why. The mother said his father did not wish to go. The boy again asked why. She said his father had seen many things in his life, and did not wish to see more.

The boy thought, if his father did not want to go across the street because he did not want to see another thing, then what things were across the street?

The boy lay on the floor breathing hard. His ball rested in the corner.

Eventually his breathing slowed and he fell asleep.

When he woke up, the room was dim. It was between day and night. Maybe now his mother would let him to play outside. Only he did not want to play anymore. He wanted to see the dead older boy.

But he could not ask to see the dead older boy. His mother would not let him, and then his father would watch him to make sure he didn't disobey.

The boy retrieved his ball from the corner and walked into the room where his mother was. Could he play outside now, since it was getting dark and the parents of the older dead boy would not see him?

The boy's mother said yes, but play quietly.

The boy walked into his front yard. There was little light

left. He saw the shape of his mother watching him from the big window. He walked under the tree and tossed the ball into the air and then caught it. He did this several times, and then he looked at the window. His mother was gone.

The boy turned toward the house across the street. He saw a woman's shape in the big window of that house. He hid behind the tree. He stood there until she disappeared. By then, the day was gone.

The boy walked to the street. He looked both ways, twice, as his mother had taught him. We live on a busy highway, she told him.

The boy saw no cars, nor did he hear them. He looked back to the big window in his house. Nothing. Then he stared again at the big window across the street. Nothing.

He ran across the road, still holding his ball. He then ran across the neighbor's yard until he reached the brick just below the big window. He ducked low enough to be out of sight.

Where might the dead older boy be? The boy was afraid to look into the big window. The mother was probably still near. But all the other windows were dark.

A light at the other end of house flicked on. The boy walked low along the brick house. He reached the window, crouched lower, remaining out of sight. He listened. He heard nothing.

The boy raised up. He looked into the window.

He jerked away, ran across the neighbor's yard, ran across the road without looking left or right.

When he reached the other side, he was breathing hard. He wanted to go inside his house. But he no longer held his ball. He looked at the road. His ball was rolling down the middle of the road.

The older dead boy's mother watched from her big window. The younger boy's mother turned away from her own.

POLARIS'S ROOM
(SWORN)

Who the woman was who was in my house, I forgot. If I ever remembered. If you don't know who she is now, how do you know if you knew who she was then?

I say the word "know" as if you know what I mean. Surely, you do. But to be clear—for without clarity, what do we have?—I shall remind you that to know someone means, if you threaten her, you know how she will react.

This is what someone taught me who once lived in my house.

But you want me to tell you what happened. Such is the purpose. I know. Perhaps you are thinking, "Get to the point." You mean that ironically, I imagine, for I am already discussing the point, am I not? The point being, when did I know what?

Why you ended that last session abruptly, I know. You told me you would suspend this activity if I did not tell you what you wished to hear.

You desire this document to support your theory. But surely you know the document can only be significant if it either reveals a truth that has escaped your theory, or demonstrates the false pretenses under which you have been laboring.

I realize you are most interested in that woman who was in my house. This subject is tedious. I have confessed to you repeatedly, one day I woke up and a woman was in my house. It's not that I saw her first thing that morning. I felt her.

You surely know what I mean.

You are walking down a street at night, and you know someone is following you. You turn around quickly, and you see no one, but you know someone is there.

You just know it, in the same way—to take another example—you know if someone is spying on you. The person, perhaps a person who lives in your house, talks to you as if she has long known you, asks you about your nightly walks, the tree you avoid, and so on, but all the while she is watching closely your every move, in order to report your activities.

That's how I knew a woman was in my house that morning, as I might know someone is following me or spying on me.

You might ask, "Why did you not immediately seek this woman out, this woman in your house, and get to the bottom of it? Inquire why she was in the house, what her disposition was, and the like?"

The answer should be obvious. I didn't pursue this woman in my house because then she would have known I was in the house.

You see, just as I knew she was in the house, even though I did not know who she was, I also knew she did not know I was in the house, and very likely did not know who I was.

I remained in the room where I sleep. I waited for this woman to appear in my room. When she did, I would find out who she was and know what to do. Essential to my plan was, I remain unknown to her.

You've made yourself very clear. This is my last chance to make

13

known what it was I did to the woman in my house whom I did not know. I also understand what will happen to me if I do not report what I did, if anything, to the woman I did not know.

Let me begin at the beginning. I woke up. A woman was in my house. I did not know this woman. She did not know I was in the house.

Exactly when this woman appeared in my room is unknown. I was still in the place of the room where I sleep, knowing that remaining in this place would keep her from knowing I was in the house.

She was standing three feet from me. She was looking in my direction. She was looking right where my eyes were. She was performing the act of, "I recognize you."

Meaning, she looked smugly satisfied.

Because I did not know her, or if I did I forgot who she was, I could not predict how she would react when I did it, if I did it.

In any case, I did what anyone would do when a woman he does not know is staring where his eyes are. I closed my eyes.

When I opened them, this woman was in the place of the room where I sleep. Her body was touching mine. I could tell by how her flesh felt she probably once had a name. I remembered that I, too, had a name.

Polaris was my name. Two made one. One made two.

I looked where her eyes were. I had to establish she no longer recognized me. Her eyes were wide-open, as before, but no smug satisfaction now. She did not know me.

I know this, because she remained in the place where I sleep a long time, a very long time, and she never knew me.

She is still there, for all I know.

If you would let me return to my house, to the place where I sleep in my house, I could tell you. I would know by feeling her flesh. Last I knew, it was no longer soft and cold. It was rough. It was rough and black and it was hot. It burned me.

No one knows how it burned me.

POLARIS'S ROOM
(THE WATCH)

I saw them do it near barbed wire. That surprised me. Soft flesh so close to such sharpness.

Then I remembered cutting was why in the first place.

There was a stump there, too, so maybe a forest once, before the saws and bulls. A tree, or the memory of one, would be right, since something growing could happen from it one day.

The old man had told me I should mark the time the blood runs down the leg. He had done so when he saw it, he said, and it had stuck in his head forever. And he was younger than I was.

There was no fence when he saw it. It was a house whose windows were broken and rooms empty. Way out in the woods, far from anywhere. No one who cared could have heard the sounds.

I heard the sounds when it was my time. I knew it was the pain and that not caring meant I would be what the old man said. And I knew she wasn't really my sister, even if we did have the eyes.

That's what I was thinking when I took out my watch, of how blue they were when she would stare out the attic window. I was waiting for the blood.

But the sounds that were the pain stabbed my hand and I dropped the watch. This had never happened before, and it would not have mattered if they hadn't heard the glass break on the stone at my foot.

They stopped what they were doing and looked toward the sound and they saw me.

They were careless with me. The barbs punctured my belly, and they put the broken watch inside me.

That's when the blood flowed, but there was no one there to mark it.

Unless the old man still had his watch. I saw him just when they were binding us together, because of our eyes, and talking about the house in the woods. He was standing where I had stood, and he was staring, and his eyes were no longer blue but solid white, like our skin, except for the red.

Now we are inside the walls and I can't see anyone marking the time and no one can hear the sounds we make when they are doing it. No one who is able to care.

BOOK III

"You are now old enough to bathe on your own," her father said.

"But the water is too deep," the girl, not yet six, replied.

"Your head will be above the water line," the father said. "You will be fine. I am making a cake for your mother. She might be coming home tonight."

"But the water will get cold," the girl said.

The father replied, "Not for a long time. It is almost boiling hot. Please get in."

"But what if the lights go out?"

"They won't. Now get in. You are dirty, and your mother will not like it."

The girl's father left the room. The girl became naked and stepped into the tub and lowered herself into the water.

The water in the porcelain tub looked white. The whiteness turned the room around it black. The girl sat in the darkness the white made. She loved the warm water on her skin. Her father was right, the water would not get cold. She leaned her head back against the rim of the old tub. She fell asleep.

She awoke choking. She had slid under the water. She heaved herself upward and coughed and spit until she caught her breath. The water was now cold, and it was no longer white. The darkness in the room did not make the white whiter. The dark was dark.

The girl cried out, "Daddy, daddy."

Her father did not come.

"Daddy."

Silence.

The girl would have to climb out of the tub on her own.

She placed her hands on either side of the tub and pulled her knees to her chest. But before she could rise from the water, a hole opened in the ceiling and through it rushed hot white light and a blur of gray and the water splashed into her eyes and it stung them and then she forced them open and above her was the man from her mother's book, giant and silvery, circle of black for a mouth, no eyes, nose, ears, in his left hand holding by the hair the head of a girl, in his right an ax so black the light turned it white.

The girl could not cry Daddy. She could scream. She screamed a scream.

The man dropped the head into the water. The water splashed into the girl's eyes. She closed them and opened them. The man was now holding her hair with his left hand and was raising the ax with his right.

A wall of smoke slid between the girl and the man from the book. The smoke was hot. It burned the girl's eyes. Someone was lifting her from the water. She was carried out of the room into the house and she was outside the house and she was in the yard. It was cool. Her father was holding her, chest-to-chest, her chin was resting on his left shoulder, like when she was a baby. She was turned away from the house. It was almost night. She was still naked.

"Daddy," she said, "the gray man from the book Mom made came through the ceiling."

"No, child, he did not," the father replied.

"He did," the girl said, "and he had an ax and he was going to cut my head off, just like in the book."

"No," he replied, "what you saw was smoke. The oven caught fire while I was in the woods looking for mushrooms. If you hadn't screamed, something terrible would have happened."

"I screamed when I saw the gray man," the girl said.

"Honey, you did not see the gray man. You saw smoke, and you screamed. You saved us. The house would've burned, you would've burned. But now the fire is out. I threw water on the oven."

The girl did not say anything. She closed her eyes and did not want her father to put her down.

He whispered in her ear, "What's happened here is grace. That's a stroke of luck that saves you from dying."

He put her down. She did not like it.

"I guess your Mom isn't coming," he said. "Let's go clean up the mess."

Then the girl's mother was home. It was later. Her mother had made a new book. It was about a girl who has a boat. The girl's name is Ella. The boat is as wide and long as a kite. It is made of the kind of paper you would use to make a kite. The boat is magic. It turns everything it touches, except Ella, into water. One day Ella is very thirsty, so she touches the boat to a book, and the book turns to water, and she drinks the water. When Ella's parents discover this—they did not know about the boat, which the gray man had given to the girl during the night—they scold her. They tell her never to turn anything to water again. But Ella is thirsty. In secret, she turns a plate into water, and then a jug, and then a chair, and a table. When Ella's parents find out, they scream at her. Ella is startled by the scream. She lets go of her boat and it drifts toward her parents. It touches them, they turn to water. Ella is sad, but drinks them anyway.

The mother read her own girl this book about Ella. At the end of the book, the girl—she was now almost nine—asked her mother, "Whatever happened to Ella?"

Her mother replied, "Ella walked all around the world, turning everything into water. She was extremely thirsty. Eventually she turned the entire world into water. But Ella had not thought that there would be no place to stand. She drowned in all of the water she had not drunk. Nothing was left but a world of water and a boat the size of a kite and made of the paper you would use to make a kite. The boat was floating on the water. But the paper became wet and heavy, and the boat sank, and then it was only the water."

"That is a sad story," the girl said.

"Perhaps," her mother replied, "but also true, for it tells us what kind of people we are. I brought you a present."

The girl's mother reached inside her coat. She was always wearing a coat now, a thick gray one. She was always cold. Out of her coat, she produced a blue paper boat, the size of two palms placed side-by-side to gather water. It floats, her mother said, and she tossed it into the air and it floated down to the floor as a boat would float down a waterfall.

Soon after that the mother left again and did not return. The girl played with the blue boat. She tossed it into the air and watched it float down to the floor.

One morning the girl woke up and the boat was gone. She

always placed the boat beside her pillow before going to sleep. But the boat was now not beside her pillow. Nor was it under her bed, nor anywhere else in her room. Nor was it in the house she lived in with her father, the house whose kitchen had blackened walls. She could not find the boat outside, either, not in the yard, not at the edge of the woods.

Where had the blue boat gone?

The girl lay down in her bed. She was sure that last night her boat had been right beside where her head now was. She did not believe in the gray man, as she once did, so she did not wonder if the gray man had taken her boat. Then she thought she might be in a dream, that all she had to do was wake up from this dream, and the boat would be right there, beside her head. She reasoned that if she closed her eyes and fell asleep in this dream, if this was a dream, then the dream she would have in this sleep would not be a dream, but reality, herself as she really was, waking up and finding her blue boat beside her.

The girl closed her eyes. They had not been closed long before she heard scratching from the kitchen. It was her father. He wrote in the mornings, with an old-timey fountain pen.

The girl opened her eyes. She looked where her boat should have been. It was not there, but she did notice a small hole at the base of the wall between her room and the bathroom. The hole was roughly a half circle, and just big enough for her blue boat to fit through.

She sprang from her bed to the wall. She lay on her stomach and looked into the hole. She expected to see the bathroom on the other side. She hoped her boat would be there.

But the girl saw darkness in the hole. She should have seen light, light from the bathroom, through whose window the morning sun shone. But she saw darkness.

What was this hole?

She wanted to reach into the hole to find out if her boat was there, but she was afraid. Anything could be in this hole. A rat, or a spider, or something else, even though she no longer believed in the gray man.

The girl wanted her blue boat very much, though. It was the last present her mother had given her, and she liked tossing it into the air and watching it float down to the floor.

The girl reached into the hole with her left hand. At first, she only went as far as her wrist. She felt nothing but cool air. Then she pushed in farther, up to her elbow. Still only cool air.

There was nothing dangerous in this hole. She reached in all the way to her shoulder. She felt something papery. But in touching this papery thing, likely her boat, she pushed it away, out of her reach. She stretched her arm as far as she could, but it remained out of her reach.

She thought, I can use a broomstick to slide this papery thing, surely my boat, toward me.

The girl removed her arm and ran into the kitchen. Her father had stopped writing. He looked sad.

"Where is a broom?" the girl said.

"In the closet," her father replied. "Why do you need a broom?"

She thought it best not to tell her father the truth. "To sweep my room," she said.

"What?" her father said. "What's gotten in to you? You've never swept your room before."

"I'm going to clean my room to cheer you up," the girl said. "I'm going to clean the entire house."

"You are a sweet girl," his father said.

The girl took the broom from the closet. She hurried back into her room.

She lay on her belly again and extended the broom handle into hole. The handle touched something. This had to be the boat. She then positioned the handle to the left of the thing and slowly tried to angle the thing back towards her.

But it slid away to the right and lost contact with the broom handle. The girl slid the handle to the right as far as she could, but it touched nothing. She slid the handle to the left as far as she could. Nothing. She slid the handle back and forth, once, twice, three times. Nothing.

Where had the boat gone?

"What are you doing?"

Had someone spoken?

"Honey, what are you doing?"

It was her father. She turned toward his voice. He was standing in the doorway. She pulled the broom from the hole and stood up.

She thought it best not to tell him the truth.

"I was sweeping," she said, "and just noticed this hole and wondered how deep it goes."

"How did that hole get there?" her father asked. "I've never noticed it before. Did you make it while you were playing?"

"No," the girl said.

"Do not lie to me," her father replied. "I hear you playing roughly in here all the time. I bet you did it while playing with that boat your mother gave you."

"No, I didn't," the girl said. "I swear."

"All you do is play with that boat," her father said. "I'm

sick of it. Give me the boat."

"I don't know where it is."

"You lost it?"

"I woke up this morning and it was gone."

"Are you lying?"

"No. I swear." Now the girl would tell the truth. "It floated into this hole."

"Impossible," his father said. "You have disappointed me again."

She started to cry. He walked out of the room.

The girl's father did not speak to her the rest of the day.

ELLA'S MEMO

Moon-glossed and arched above the swells, my breasts. Sick, you stare. "Look," I say. "They shine." Unclothed you reach. I back-dive away, and the surf lurches dark. You bury your erection in the foam. The fishermen cast their sinkers, and with their beams they find the tightening lines. The light falls short of my strokes.

BOOK IV

Ella's twin brother had the night terrors. After midnight, Otto, who looked just like his sister, sprang from bed, screamed through the house. Something terrible was chasing him. Only he could see it. He ran from room to room, banged into furniture and walls, crouched in a corner, pointed to the air, sobbed and screamed.

Ella tried to wake Otto up. She ran behind him screaming "wake up! wake up!" She hovered over Otto while he was in the corner, and she screamed again "wake up! wake up!" She grabbed Otto by the shoulders and shook him hard as she could, and still screamed for her brother to wake up.

But Otto never woke up when Ella did these things. Eventually Ella grew exhausted. She collapsed on the floor near her sobbing and screaming brother, and she fell asleep, in spite of the terrible noise. She woke in the same corner. It was morning. Her brother was gone.

Ella stumbled to the room where she and Otto slept. Otto was in the bed sleeping. Ella crawled into the bed beside him and tried to go back to sleep. She never did, since she was so sad about her brother's terror, and so curious about what he saw.

When the terror would seize her brother, Ella could never predict. Sometimes it happened that Otto ran screaming through the dark house two or three nights in a row. Then he slept soundly for a month before having another nightmare, and then go another month, sometimes several, before having another. During these long periods between terrors, Ella forgot about Otto's troubles.

Then Ella and Otto turned nine.

Everyone said, "I know they look just alike, but I can't believe they are twins, they are so different." People had been saying that for as long as Ella could remember.

But Ella knew she and Otto were exactly alike for just as much time as they were different. Yes, during the day they might say different words or walk in different rooms or love separate trees, but at night, when they were asleep side-by-side in the bed, lying on their backs with their hands folded across their chests, they were exactly the same. And when Ella screamed while chasing a screaming Otto, they were exactly the same.

People didn't notice this, or they forgot, maybe because of what happened when Ella and Otto were much younger, too young to know the difference between being old and being young.

Ella and Otto were taking a bath. The soapy water had turned gray in the old porcelain tub. No sun shone into the room. It was raining outside. The rain pelted the roof so hard Ella and Otto could hardly hear the bathwater slosh.

The twins had been in the bath a long time. The water was cold. The time had come to climb out. They were too small to do this on their own.

The twins screamed for their parents to help them, but no one could hear them, the rain was so loud. They screamed louder. No one came. The rain pounded harder. Ella and Otto shivered.

"Out," Ella said to Otto.

"Out," Otto said to Ella.

Ella tried to lift herself out of the tub. She slipped on the porcelain and splashed back into the water.

Otto tried to lift himself out of the tub. He also failed.

Otto cried. Ella did not.

Drops from above hit the water. Otto stopped crying and looked up. Ella looked up.

There was a crack in the ceiling. The drops pelted the wide-open eyes of the twins. They lowered their heads.

Otto cried.

Ella did not.

What happened next depends on who was telling the story.

Some say Ella hit Otto in the face, and screamed "stop," and then pushed Otto under the water and stepped on him and pushed herself over the edge of the tub and fell to the ground and screamed in pain. The parents did hear this scream. They rushed to the room. Ella was lying on the floor, naked and wet and crying. At first, the parents could not see Otto, but then they found him under the gray water. They pulled him out. His face was blue. He was not breathing. The mother flung him over her shoulder and struck his back. Otto spit out water, gasped and coughed, and breathed again, and the blue left his face.

Others say that Otto slapped Ella in the face, screamed "cry," and then slammed Ella's head into the edge of the tub, and Ella sunk under the water, and then Otto climbed onto Ella, and pushed himself out of the tub, and into the floor, where he screamed after striking his head on the floor. The parents heard this scream, ran in, found Otto writhing on the floor and Ella unconscious under the water. The father pulled Ella from the water, flung her over his shoulder, hit her on the back, and nothing happened. The father then lay Ella on the floor beside her writhing, screaming brother. Ella woke up.

Still others believe that on this cold day when the roof leaked—and the river flooded the town—the twins had a fight, and this fight showed that they were very different from one another.

On the day Ella and Otto turned nine, everyone was saying, more than usual, "These two are so different, it's hard to believe they are twins."

The gifts given to Ella and Otto were based on this belief.

Ella received a black skirt, while Otto received a white pair of pants. Ella, because she liked to carve soap, got a pocket knife, and Otto the art-lover opened a box of brushes. Ella's last present, from her parents, was a small bronze hourglass. The last present Otto received, also from the parents, was a silver kite.

Otto said, "I will fly my kite right now."

Ella thought to herself, "Otto has not had a night terror in a long time."

Ella said, "I will help you."

Ella followed Otto. Just before they reached the door leading outside, Ella said, "I brought my knife." She opened her knife. The blade gleamed. "Feel how sharp it is."

Otto ran his thumb lightly down the edge of the blade. But not lightly enough.

"Ouch!" Otto cried.

Blood from the cut dripped onto his silver kite, which he had laid on the floor before testing Ella's blade.

Ella said, "Get mother to bandage your thumb."

By the time the mother had bandaged Otto's thumb, the sky was dark. Otto would not fly his kite.

Ella and Otto crawled in bed together. Ella was glad for this, since she and her twin would now be exactly the same for the next twelve hours.

The twins lay on their backs, crossed their arms over their chests, and fell asleep.

Otto sprang out of bed. He was screaming.

Ella sprang out of bed and stood very close to her brother. She screamed "wake up, wake up!"

Otto did not hear. He ran out of the room screaming. Something terrible was chasing him. Ella was right behind him, screaming for him to wake up, wake up.

Otto ran from room to room, screaming. Ella followed, screaming.

Otto reached the door leading to the outside. He tried to open it, it was locked. He turned around, he was facing Ella. He crouched by the door, pointed to the air, screamed and sobbed.

Ella grabbed Otto by the shoulders and shook him. "Wake up! Wake up!"

Otto screamed and sobbed. Ella squeezed her brother harder than ever. She squeezed and squeezed.

"What do you see? What do you see?" she screamed.

Otto could not answer. Otto could not breathe.

All Otto could do was see, and he saw a shape inches from his face, and he felt hands on his neck, and he could not breathe, and then he could not see.

Ella exhausted herself. She fell asleep beside Otto.

Ella woke up. The night had gone.

Ella saw Otto's kite beside the door. The blood stain had dried. It was no longer red but brown.

Ella noticed a foot beside the stain, a bare foot. This was Otto's foot. Then Ella remembered. Otto had had a night terror.

Ella followed the foot to the leg, the leg to the belly and the chest, and then she lighted on Otto's face. It was blue. He was not breathing.

Ella was no longer curious about what Otto was seeing during his night terrors.

Ella stood up. Otto did not.

Ella knew now she could make her brother do exactly as she did. They would be the same all the time.

Ella picked up the kite. She saw her knife, which had been under the kite. She picked it up, too.

Ella stepped over his brother, unlocked the door, and walked outside. There would be plenty of time to make her brother do exactly as she did.

For now, she would fly his kite. If it got tangled in a tree, she would cut the string and leave it there.

There would be no mystery as to how to get it down.

THE COLLECTED WORKS
OF OTTO WILBUR, PART 1

About porcelain and blood, before marriage, he wrote sonnets.
Tantalizing, his teacher called them. In the beginning his wife
praised. He misplaced his ring. The teacher morphed into a
woman. She gilded as quickly as the wife the actual, blanched.

— G.R.S. Eisenhower

ODDITY

Elvis was born thirty-five minutes after his stillborn twin Jesse.

When Elvis was a baby, a tornado killing two-hundred only missed him by half a mile.

Via Oz, David Lynch linked cyclone and Elvis in *Wild at Heart*, which starred Nicolas Cage, who married Elvis's daughter Lisa Marie, with whom he quarreled on his yacht. She tossed her $65,000 engagement ring into the Pacific.

Unlike other children of celebrities (Brando's daughter Cheyenne, for instance, who hung herself), Lisa Marie avoided her dad's depression, which he shared with his cousin Abraham Lincoln, along with somnambulism, an impoverished Southern upbringing, and the premature death of a beloved mother.

White snakeroot killed Lincoln's mother Nancy.

Elvis purchased two electric mixers for his mother Gladys, one for each side of the kitchen.

King and President descended from Isaiah Harrison, born in England in 1666.

Did Elvis and Lincoln inherit their depressive genes from him?

Manic depression has poisoned the Wilbur line, half-broke fanatics and alcoholics wandering the grim Appalachians. Self-hatred harries me, as it did Elvis.

Love me love me: the scorch of his songs.

Elvis romanced Natalie Wood, who drowned under

suspicious circumstances involving her husband.

Her daughter Natasha played in Lynch's *Lost Highway*.

If Elvis had starred in the movie of *West Side Story*, as planned, he and Wood, who did star, might have married, and Wood might still be alive.

Rita Moreno, Wood's co-star, dated Elvis to make Marlon Brando, whose infidelity turned her suicidal, jealous.

"I am the Marlon Brando of DVD," Lynch admitted.

David Bowie plays FBI Agent Jeffries in *Twin Peaks: Fire Walk with Me*. Thought dead, he staggers into headquarters and announces, in a southern drawl not un-reminiscent of Elvis, that he will not talk about Judy.

Bowie and Elvis were born on January 8. Both released albums in 1972, *The Rise and Fall of Ziggy Stardust and the Spiders from Mars* and *Elvis Now*.

"Seeing Is Believing," a cut from the Elvis disc, was written by Red West, who later played in *Goodbye Solo*, set in the city where I live. Also dwelling here is the woman I was dating when I attended a Bowie concert in '87. She and I were fighting that night, over how I can't be trusted because I'll do anything for adulation. She tore off a necklace I had given her and hurled it into the audience below. She shoved her way to the stage. There she saw Bowie in the wings, just before the show's second half. He looked at her and smiled.

I completed this last sentence the evening of January 10, 2016. When I awoke the next morning, appeared in *The New York Times* the prose-poem of Jon Pareles: "David Bowie Dies at 69; Star Transcended Music, Art and Fashion." Aside from sex—was the androgyne adept?—"69" symbolizes Bowie's reversals. David Jones from South London morphs into ethereal Ziggy, who in turn transforms into Aladdin Sane, reasonable conjurer and "lad insane." A red and blue lightning bolt splits Aladdin's melancholy face. (Elvis's trademark is a bolt crowned by "TCB," Taking Care of Business.) Bowie's death age is more than his death age. He is the Star Man. "I'm stepping through the door / And I'm floating in a most peculiar way / And the stars look very different today." Transcendence of more than "Music, Art and Fashion."

Your doors of perception: cleanse. Pass "one-hundred-thousand miles."

These visions rare as Elvis-sightings on an earth boring and botched. Pressed to your chair, you are never not channel-surfing reruns in the thousands.

Bowie wanted to meet anti-gravity Elvis, who wore zoot suits and eyeliner to barn dances. In '72, Bowie flew from London to New York to see the gaudy King in the Garden. He sat near the stage, his rooster-comb neon-orange, ghostly pale his face. The glam-meet never came off.

Liberace, whose twin also died at birth, encouraged Elvis's bling. Both musicians pined for their missing halves and abandoned themselves to living for two. Hence the emptiness, the excess.

Had they met, Bowie would not have admitted cocaine, nor Elvis meth.

I confess booze. Call my pain Gnostic: this darkling stretch *can't* be all there is. Call it a hole in the soul (the ghost) unfillable in the sub-lunar. What makes one whole, past one-hundred-thousand-miles.

I was drunk at the Bowie concert where my date broke her chain. I've been drinking ever since, corn liquor (from an old fruit jar) when I can get it. I'm heavy depressed, and I *will* do anything for praise.

Elvis tee-totaled. Robert Mitchum, who inspired the King's coif, did not. In *Thunder Road*, he hotrods Appalachian moonshine beyond the revenuers' reach.

Springsteen borrowed the title. I heard him perform the song in Charlotte in '85. First time I ever got loaded, on Beam and Sun Drop, and I had no date, I was a senior in high school, and a football star, and had bedded a doting sophomore, and since that time I have been sad.

The last number of Bowie before an audience was "Changes." "I watch the ripples change their size / But never leave the stream / Of warm impermanence," it goes.

Elvis's final croon: "My Baby Left Me."

PORN

Coitus perpetually a mouse-click from your eyes, you think about nothing else, but coitus a click from your eyes. The cosmetic genitalia so close to the real, you think you can transcend your own grim privates, rise to the pleasure of repeated pleasure.

A machine is this and no that, this and no that, this and no that.

"Life is just one damned thing after another," Toynbee wrote. Civilizations, he believed, decay from within.

Thomas Monson, head of the Mormon Church, calls pornography the "bark beetle" to the elm of humankind. Monson worked as an advertiser for the *Deseret News*.

When interviewed by this paper, I said: "If you create a narrative that's so far removed from yourself and your circumstances, that will lead to sorrow."

For his service on the National Executive Board of the Boy Scouts, Monson received a Silver Beaver.

I attended Boy Scout Camp, and I shared a bunk with Joe, a stranger. The first night, he said, "I hate pornos where you see the stretch marks."

My friend Shane, no Scout, led me to his brother Billy's room. It was dark and crimson, with a poster of Linda Ronstadt on the wall. Model jeeps appeared everywhere. A tiny plastic skeleton leaned against one. Under Billy's mattress were a *Climax*, whose cover depicted a penis inserted into a woman's anus, and a *Rouge*, where a bearded man touched a vagina with his tongue. "Let's go to the basement," Shane said.

Last summer I toured the Utah desert in an off-road SUV. Lemuel, the driver I hired, weighed two-fifty and sported a shovel-head beard. The stunts he performed enlivened the rocks. He raised hell in the seventies but converted to Mormonism, quit drinking, raised twelve children. When he saw a Jack Daniels mini in my seat—fallen from my pocket—he shouted, "Never forget the murder of Joseph Smith is essential to our faith." Then he pointed to the west. A cave was there. For fifty extra, he would take me.

Shane called his basement the cavern. It smelled of detergent and glue and motor oil. In the center, two black leather sofas faced each other on a square of black shag. The lamp suspended above was red and globular. Shane and I each sat down on a sofa. The women in the mags looked bored. Their tans touched the pearl-white circling their aureoles and spreading like wings from their pubic V's. The faces of the men remained unseen.

Joseph Smith enjoyed forty wives. Nathan Mitchell portrayed him in *Joseph Smith: Prophet of the Restoration*. Mitchell has acted in several Mormon films and leads troubled youths on retreats in the Arizona wilderness.

Willem Dafoe played Christ. He was also expelled from high school for making a porn film. "Anything to get out of [Wisconsin]," he exclaimed. Dafoe enjoyed an early sexual encounter with Wendy Witt, whose parents "were relaxed about sex because they didn't want us to be fucked up about it."

Wendy O. Williams is who I watched at the age when Dafoe was filming sex. In the video for "The Damned," O. Williams stands atop a school bus speeding through the desert. She wears a black bikini top, a black loin cloth, high black boots. Metal spikes thrust from her black elbow pads, and her bleached Mohawk stands four inches high. The bus crashes through a wall of stacked televisions.

Before her punk fame, O. Williams appeared in the porn film *Candy Goes to Hollywood*. Her character, named Wendy Williams, competes in a talent show. From her vagina she shoots ping pong balls, while her male partner, dressed like drum major, tries to catch them in his mouth.

My testicles, by the time I had finished the *Rouge*, hurt.

At the age of forty-eight, a tormented O. Williams walked into the woods near her Connecticut home, fed acorns to squirrels, and shot herself to death with a pistol. In her suicide note, she wrote "much of the world makes no sense, but my feelings about what I am doing ring loud and clear to an inner ear and a place where there is no self, only calm."

I am forty-eight.

Porn, regular as a mechanical pen or a gun, goads and numbs. Unperceived goes the discord in the players.

What was occurring behind Shane's jeans, I could not fathom. "Have you ever stroked it?" I asked. "No," he said. "I used suntan lotion once," I admitted.

Shane is now an evangelical minister.

Our senior year in high school, O. Williams released the single "It's My Life," in which she wails "shining from the roof."

SMACK

If you haven't read *Hamlet*, you've read *Hamlet*. How you look for something, and nothing is there, or something else that should not, in your mind, exist.

In 1946, Alfred Hitchcock asked Cary Grant to play Hamlet. "To be or not to be" would be delivered from a psychiatrist's couch and updated to "What the hell do I do now?"

Grant, born poor Archie Leach and believing from age nine to adulthood his mother had abandoned him when really his father had secretly committed her to an insane asylum, refused the role. He said he was too old.

In reality he couldn't endure the first line, "Who's there?"

Grant said, "Everybody wants to be Cary Grant. Even I want to be Cary Grant."

In high school, I staged the final scene of *Hamlet*. I lip-synched John Gielgud speaking Hamlet on a record, and Goler, from Turkey, mouthed Sebastian Shaw's Horatio. I wore a cheerleading uniform, an "H" pinned to my chest. My Hamlet died, and Goler mouthed flights of angels sing me to my rest. Then he pretended to stomp on my head. The class laughed.

Shaw would have favored this comic Horatio. In *Return of the Jedi*, he played Darth Vader unmasked. His hairless flesh is dead fish and scars mottle his pate. The action figure of this character is extremely valuable.

Hitchcock cast Gielgud, a wartime Air Warden, in *Secret*

Agent, about a man forced into espionage but reluctant to act. (T.S. Eliot was an Air Warden; Gielgud later recorded the poet's book about cats.) Smitten with female lead Madeleine Carroll, Hitchcock grew bored of Gielgud and filmed him indifferently.

Carroll was the type that obsessed Hitchcock: an "English girl, looking like a schoolteacher, [who] is apt to get into a cab with you and, to your surprise, she'll probably pull a man's pants open."

Grace Kelly epitomized fire under ice. Though she insisted Hitchcock treated her "like a porcelain doll," in *Dial M for Murder* he subjected her to a brutal beating scene that covered her in bruises.

"Torture the women!" Hitchcock exclaimed.

Kelly's weaker double was Tippi Hedren. The director controlled what she wore, the color of her hair, her diet. He hired spies to ensure compliance, and he once sent a doll of Hedren lying in a coffin to her five-year-old daughter Melanie Griffith.

How Jimmy Stewart's Scotty viciously transforms Novak's Judy into Madeleine predicts Hitchcock's warping of Tippi and summons Hamlet's idealism.

If the world is not exactly as Hamlet desires, he must convert it or kill himself.

Idealism says no to what is. Nothing would exist without idealism. The "or" that harries Hamlet, to be *or* not, is not as tragic as the "and," not to be *and* be.

Hedren surely hated Kelly as a drowned woman, such as Ophelia, would a wounded sea nymph.

Puck in *Midsummer Night's Dream* heard an unharmed mermaid express, while riding on a "dolphin's back," such "a

dulcet and harmonious breath / That the rude sea grew civil"
and "certain stars shot madly from their spheres."

Gielgud, who played Oberon in '31 (and so required the
"juice" of "hateful fantasies"), won an Oscar for his acerbic
butler in *Arthur*, the '81 comedy starring Dudley Moore.

Moore's '79 film *10*, featuring the cornrowed Bo Derek,
is about idealism's torture. You don't possess your brain's
beauties, the longing palsies you; you do, disappointment does.

10 was playing on a television in Goler's parents' bedroom
when I first felt a girl's breast. This was 1980. I was thirteen.
Gina pulled me down to the bed, and she kissed me, and she
placed my left hand on her right breast, and she put her hand
on my crotch. Goler rushed into the room screaming, "Kopec-
tu-shock-yay!" He later said this was Turkish for "fuck-shit-
bitch."

The day I mouthed Gielgud's Hamlet an old girlfriend,
Uriel, visited the school. The last time I had seen her was
two years earlier, during the trial of a young American named
Dieter. After dating Uriel three times he broke into her house,
tied her and her family up, and attempted to rape her. He failed,
because she convinced him his hatred for his mother had made
him violent toward women. He fell to the floor and wept. He
pled insanity and was sentenced to two years. Uriel feared that
once released he would hound her again. She and her family
moved away, and she changed her name.

Now, two years later, minutes after my performance, she
was Uriel again, since Dieter was on death row for drowning
another woman. Uriel never revealed the name she had assumed.
She told me my performance of Hamlet was irreplaceable, and
she missed me while she was someone else. That was the last

time I saw her.

Fifteen years later, I realize she kindled my soul, though I broke up with her after touching Gina's breast. I have tried to locate her on the web. No one going by her name has appeared.

No one is who Hamlet thinks Ophelia is. Hamlet asks her if he can rest his head on her lap. No, she says. Did she think he meant "country matters?" (Country puns "cunt.") She thinks nothing. "That's a fair thought to lie between maids' legs." "What is?" "No thing," Hamlet replies, implying the vagina, in Elizabethan England a lack, an absence, a zero, O, the hole.

Ophelia, who would have been played by a boy, hollows the play. Everyone else who dies has it coming. The milty stream soaks to the bone innocent Ophelia.

Fast-talking Uriel would have called that last sappy. Behind every tree is Dieter or Hitch who torments the world into masturbatory figments.

When I taught *Hamlet*, I remembered my old professor, Eisenhower. He said "If Freud is right even the author's pencil is a substitute for the phallus. Anyway, let's . . . ." Eisenhower noticed a small nub of chalk on the seminar table. He picked it up long-ways between thumb and forefinger and held it up to his class. It was a quarter inch. The class laughed. I tried the joke during my class on *Hamlet*. The men were agog, the women mortified. I emailed the class later to claim I had a cold and consumed too much Nyquil.

A year later I was on heavy lithium. While explaining Freud's Oedipal Theory to another class on *Hamlet*, I felt my voice leave my mouth and hover three feet to the left of my head. The voice said, "The infant never wants to stop sucking its mother's breast. Daddy, who also likes mother's breast, pulls baby off, shouts, 'those titties are mine!'"

Yesterday I read the essay of a woman in my most recent class on *Hamlet*. She had spent the weekend walking around the Museum of Modern Art, and she had gotten so chafed between her thighs she felt like she had been "fucked by a ghost."

If Uriel would appear in one of my classes, I would become something other than the sesquipedalian man I now am. I would speak only what I know, and she knows what I mean, and she loves it, and we are lovely and quiet.

Skulls are the quietest objects on earth.

David Tennant, Dr. Who, uttered "poor Yorick" to the actual skull of composer André Tchaíkowsky.

When Daniel Day-Lewis played Hamlet, he saw on stage the ghost of his own recently-deceased father. He exited left and wept in the wings. He has not tread the boards since.

Hamlet, who did not walk off the stage mid-performance, turned his obsession for self-murder into puns, paradoxes, hyperboles, and ironies, on clouds, gardens, acting, music, vaginas, death's undiscovered country, nuns, fencing, what a skeleton dreams. He most loved riffing on what he was doing but did not want to, and what he was not doing but wanted to. Not one minute is what he would like, but every single second is meaningful.

French actress Sarah Bernhardt played Hamlet in 1899. Was he a girl raised as a boy? Is his mind so capacious it encompasses male and female?

Virginia Woolf, haunted by London and drawing from Coleridge, believed that Shakespeare possessed an androgynous mind, "naturally creative, incandescent and undivided."

Hamlet, asunder, enjoyed all but the last.

So torn he could barely move, Coleridge observed, "I have a smack of Hamlet myself."

Samuel Taylor wrote the screenplay for *Vertigo*, for which Hitch initially wanted Grant, but Stewart ended up afraid of heights. Grant's "The Cat," guilty of a rash of recent transgressions, prances over rooftops in *To Catch a Thief*, co-starring Kelly. She is sangfroid until she "plunges her mouth into Cary Grant's."

In '58, Grant played opposite Eva Marie Saint in *North by Northwest*. It is about a man trapped in a city of mirrors. Marie Saint, whose name is Eve, shatters the glass. She offers her hand, icy and burning.

Southerly fans the wind, defying augury. I am only crazy sometimes.

SWANK

Gangrene is what Keats witnessed. He studied medicine.

The saw rips the femur, the patient bites the cane.

I saw one, leather-wrapped, in London, teeth-marked from epochs back.

Keats claimed to be a billiard ball, a whale, a baited bear. But the cropped child he could not enter.

Pool, when drinking, I play passably.

Fast Eddie whips Gleason's Fats twenty-four hours solid. In a lull, Fats combs his hair, and he washes his hands. He dons his suit jacket. He then requests the talc. "Let's play some pool," he says.

Fats' preferred aesthetic was slow art. Jonathon Keats put pinhole cameras, century-long exposure times, throughout Berlin. In 2114, the pictures will be processed.

The next year will see the release of *One-Hundred Years*, starring John Malkovich. It depicts three versions of the future. Louis XIII Cognac financed the production. An executive describes the film, a tragi-comic mix, as "a tribute to the mastery of time."

The night he cut me, Professor Eisenhower was drunk on cognac. We were strangers. He was fifty and rotund. I, nineteen, medium. "Well, old sport, when are we going drinking?" he asked. "Say the word," I said.

The interiors of his rancher were dingy yellow, empty

of photographs, and smelled like chicken. I got so wasted I thought I was not wasted. "We would eat tuna tonight, but too much is bad for my diet," was Eisenhower's innuendo. He toasted literary companionship, "two men getting balls naked and quoting sonnets."

I am now an English professor.

In the middle of the night, I vomit in the toilet. I return to bed.

Insomnia and depression are primary causes of Cyclical Vomiting Syndrome.

Malkovich directed *Balm in Gilead*. Earlier, he starred in *True West*. Later, Phillip Seymour Hoffman did. Hoffmann died of heroin. He abandoned his young daughters and a son.

My daughter's name is Ursula. She is thirteen.

God's mercy gone, Jeremiah asks, is there "no balm in Gilead?"

"The day my fiancée died, my students gave me that," Eisenhower said of a bust of the Bard. "His daughter dead, Lear wails, 'Never, never, never, never.'"

One critic called Gleason "a giant, aggrieved Lear." Another said Art Carney possessed the "imagination and pathos of yesterday's most eloquent loser, Charlie Chaplin."

Chaplin married Eugene O'Neill's daughter Oona. She was eighteen and he was fifty-four.

Eisenhower stared at me like I was an animal he wanted to understand. "Innocence wrested from me," he roared. He rose up. With a steak knife, he cut my left wrist. He saw blood and disappeared into the back of his house.

I heard music. It was Frank Sinatra, singing "My Way."

I left Eisenhower's house, but I did not turn off the lights.

Sinatra tried to marry Marilyn Monroe, to protect her. She said no.

Monroe was an orphan.

John Keats was an orphan. He was a "sick eagle looking at the sky."

SEXUAL ORGANS

Another time just when I arrive at a party some guy with a pierced penis is standing in the middle of the room. His penis is stretched to his knees. He has tied one end of a string to the gold loop pierced through the head, and he has tied the other end to the handle of a full green jug of wine.

He looks like it doesn't even hurt.

Everyone, women included, hands him a five dollar bill and then kind of walks away, and he just stands there, naked from the waist down, his penis stretched to hell.

I watch him untie the string. His penis snaps back like a bungee cord.

Low on money later I room with a guy who sleeps in a t-shirt and nothing else. Mornings he gets up and shuffles into the living room and sits naked on the couch. Lights up a cigarette. Watches TV.

His testicles are too big for his penis.

One time I am cooking beans. I am wearing shorts and a t-shirt and socks. No shoes.

This man is fat, he likes wrestling.

From behind he grabs me around the waist. "You are going down!" he bellows. In a kidding way, but also not.

I whirl around, break his grip, bear-hug him. I lift him up, I slip on the linoleum, smack, my head on the stove.

I come to.

He says, "Fuck, man, you ok?"

"Fuck yes, man, leave me alone."

I wobble to the hospital. I vomit.

The doctor holds me overnight.

I sleep, I wake.

The man is sitting on the edge of my bed. He reveals a can of beer, and he cracks it open.

Still later I find myself at a woman's house on Saturday night and she is in my philosophy class and we are sitting on the couch and she tells me she told a friend I am a walking orgasm and then she French kisses me and my penis grows hard and I settle in for a night of French-kissing and nothing else and so a case of blue balls.

But she slides her hand down my pants and she is rubbing my penis and I am about to ejaculate and so I remove her hand and put my hand up her dress and touch with my index and middle fingers her vagina lips, which are warm and moist.

Stop, she whispers, and I think, I've gone too far, but she says, Come up to my bedroom, and I do and we are standing beside her bed, and she slides out of her dress, it is blue, and she takes off her bra and her breasts are big and round and pale and her nipples are hard. Touch my breasts, she says, and I fondle them, I kiss them, I am going to ejaculate, and so I stop.

I pull my shirt over my head, slowly, to show off my body, I am an avid weightlifter.

Let me see the rest of you, she says, and I take off all my clothes and she does too, and we are standing naked and my penis is about to explode, and I look at her vagina, blonde and soft, a perfect V, and I think, I bet she's looking at my penis, my penis is not big.

I also think, we are going to fuck, and I will ejaculate within seconds.

I say, This is like that scene in that movie and she says, What? and I say, That movie about a boxer, when he and his girlfriend make love he undresses her and just stands and looks at her. Oh, she says, and then, You are so good-looking.

I lead her by the hand to the bed, just like the boxer in the movie, and I lay her down on her back, just like the boxer, and I crawl on top, and I don't kiss her, no, I adjust by body to where my penis is near her vagina, she spreads her legs wide, that is sexy and nearly makes me ejaculate. I slide my penis into her vagina, it is warm and wet and alive. I pull out and ejaculate on her soft, pale belly.

Not even one stroke.

I am embarrassed.

I say, God, you don't know what you do to me, implying, You are so sexy and beautiful you made me ejaculate far faster than I would have otherwise.

She could be quiet and make me self-conscious, but she lies.

I loved it, too, she says, I am in love with you.

I have only known her three days, and I say, I have always loved you, which is the kind of lie people of faith commit when they pray.

FINIS

surrealism for cowards
oceans incarnadine
the planet in the
absinthe
glottis
in the
star
falls
Blake's
Urthona into
female and male
one made two made one
Adam Kadmon Self Polaris

BOOK V

He exits the audition.

A woman he does not know says, "You study philosophy."

"Yes," he replies.

She has seen him in Eisenhower's philosophy class.

Her name is Ella.

His is Otto.

"Eisenhower," Ella observes, "believes Jacobi constructed a castle too gigantic."

"So," Otto adds, "he squatted lovely in a hovel by the moat."

They should share a meal. Neither is hungry. They walk to the lake.

Ella is crying. Her boyfriend left her for a psychiatrist.

Otto found his last girlfriend in bed with a man whose job he can't remember.

"I won't get over it," Ella confesses. "I think about ending it all."

"Though the person you are now loves the psychiatrist," Otto replies," you will change into the person who does not."

That reminds Ella of what Eisenhower thinks about appearance.

"Wasn't it apparition?" Otto asks.

Ella tells Otto her address. Come for a visit.

Three days later, Otto knocks on the door. Ella answers.

She is holding a book and wearing a blue dress.

"The part you wanted is no longer vacant," she says, and guides him inside.

ELLA'S MEMO

Where you claim you go, I drive. I don't find you not there. The ice of witnessing your absence, would be justified anguish's numbness. Are you not fucking your former student? Peroxide, January tan, flirts with her own dad. The light box, you thought, absolved you. On my bed you left it. For depression. It burns me askance. Darken and ascend, raise over my breasts my camisole. But you shout from below, your errand. The car vibrates the joists. For your vanishing, I burn.

THE COLLECTED WORKS
OF OTTO WILBUR, PART 3

The pole star's unheard harmonies, colder and more aloof
than God: this is Van Sant's last day.

— G.R.S. Eisenhower

DEPP

Eisenhower quit teaching and pushed to Alaska, where he took over his dead father's fishing business.

When Eisenhower claimed "Gloria" as his favorite song, a student asked, "Jim's or Van's?" Eisenhower, who resembles Hunter S. Thompson, replied, "Smith's," and drew on his Camel.

Patti Smith asked Johnny Depp what inspired Jack Sparrow. "Somebody once asked [Hunter S. Thompson], 'What is the sound of one hand clapping, Hunter?', and he smacked him."

In *Black Mass*, Depp at fifty doubles Jack Nicholson, star of *The Shining*, at seventy-seven.

Young Nicholson plays in *The Raven*. Poe calls the bird, "prophet still, if bird or devil!"

Tim Burton mulls a biopic of the poet, Depp to star.

In *Depp Starts Here*, Murray Pomerance contrasts the Maltese Falcon, which "seems a bird we could take in hand," with the "untouchability" of Depp's acting. Depp is "a swath of light passing across our eyes."

A philosophy professor of mine who adored Bogart said, "To say, 'I am a nihilist,' refutes nihilism." He also mocked a colleague for getting the last line of *Maltese Falcon* wrong. "It's 'stuff dreams are made *of*,' not 'on.'"

In his fantasy production of *The Tempest*, essayist Richard Rodriguez would cast the epicene Depp as the monster Caliban.

"No fish scales, no seaweed, no webbed fingers, no claws, no vaudeville. No clothes."

I teach Rodriguez. The brightest student was Latina and proud of her cleavage and looked like Winona Ryder and sat in the front row.

I saw Ryder sharing a hotdog with Depp. A black leather jacket covered his tattoo, "Winona Forever." "She's going through a lot right now," Depp claimed. "I wish I could just kiss away the pain . . . . If she, you know, I don't know what I'd do." Depp took Ryder's virginity. "So he'll always be in my heart. Forever. Kind of funny that word." After Winona dumped him, Johnny altered the ink to "Wino Forever."

Ryder refuses to reunite with Depp on screen. She condemns his romance with Amanda Heard, twenty-three years his junior.

Heard and Depp married in February of 2015. Heard filed for divorce fifteen months later. She accused Depp of abuse. Depp denied the charge.

Roman Polanski directed Depp in *The Ninth Gate*. The actor's seedy antiquary traffics satanic volumes. Polanski shot the movie in France. If he had filmed in America, he would have been arrested for raping a thirteen-year-old girl.

Eisenhower lives in Arctic Barrow. He is the one who sails the boats, the buccaneer. He sent a Polaroid of himself with a lithesome young woman in a white string bikini. Her hair is short, like a boy's. In the distance, an iceberg shines.

Smith appears androgynous on the cover of *Horses*. "Gloria" opens the album. Smith confessed "I don't like being pinned down and I'll do what the fuck I want." Also, "When I look at the crucifixion of Clinton, I look at the crucifixion of my generation."

Nicholson will always be on Clinton's side, because the President is someone who fucks.

The exterior lights at *The Shining*'s end weakly reach for the edge of the hedge maze. Within, Nicholson, in whose house Polanski allegedly raped, pursues his son with an axe.

The film is an homage to innocence.

Eisenhower has Parkinson's. The woman before the ice is his nurse. There are pentagrams in his walls.

GODZILLA

Godzilla does not live in the now. I've witnessed him not.

Go to Kyoto. Zen. Gary Snyder, the poet: "You sit, and you sweep the garden." Somewhere Basho, the cuckoo's cry.

Into my heart please sing, bird being a bird being a bird. I am desire alone, what hurt happened, what next.

The monk facing crosses his legs. Focus on your breath. I count ten. I count ten. My back tightens, bells far away, and barking, I want beer, unending is the quarrel with my wife.

We push to Tokyo. *Shin Godzilla*, the creature's thirty-first, plays. Japanese only, no subtitles. I am nostalgic for mindlessness, I am dying to see it. My wife and daughter fear confusion and look to Kabuki. "But it's a goddamn monster flick. Easy to follow. Might as well be silent."

The politicians talk in conference rooms, offices, board rooms, warehouses, hangars, riversides. Godzilla in the bay arouses maelstroms. The men talk.

Haruo Nakajima first played Go-jira, Gorilla-Whale. Between scenes in the one-hundred-forty-degree suit of rubber, he unzips and fires up cigarettes. He holds a black belt in judo and choreographs the fights.

With computers, "they can create any monster," he says, but it "is different from having someone act as Godzilla."

Critic Michael Atkinson believes "the artificialia of fantastic imagery—the zipper on the monster suit, as it were—

has a distinctive, instantly antiquated lustre that seamless visual effects cannot match."

When technology eclipsed Nakajima, he worked in a bowling alley.

Herman Melville served as a pin boy in Honolulu. He reached the lanes via a jumped whaler, life among cannibals, orgies, a mutiny, beachcombing, jail.

Melville published *Moby-Dick; or, The Whale* in 1851. Within two years Admiral Perry's black ships thrust into Tokyo's bay and forced commerce at cannon-point.

From Perry to Hiroshima historians argue is a devious line.

In 1951 Ray Bradbury published "The Fog Horn." An ancient reptilian sea-creature mistakes the horn for wailings of its own kind and rises from the depths lonely and longing. The movie *Beast from 20,000 Fathoms*, '53, surfaced from this tale. The sorrowful monster inspired Toho Studios to create Godzilla in '54. Bradbury's story impressed John Huston, who hired the writer for his '56 film of *Moby-Dick*.

I have a black belt in Tae-Kwon-Do. I am a ferocious sparer, though slow. I break bricks. I fracture my wrist. I began the sport when I drove my daughter, then five, to her first class. In the parking lot, she cried. I bought her popcorn from a convenience store. The butter shined on her hands, I took the lesson instead.

The Golden Apples of the Sun is the title of Bradbury's collection containing "The Fog Horn." The phrase is from Yeats. "The Song of Wandering Aengus." I filmed my young daughter reciting the poem. Sing-song-y and giggling, head-fires and glimmering girls.

The professor who alerted me to the Yeats poem was

sardonic and gentle, very Southern, a runner. He conjured fever images while teaching Welty's "The Recital." He suffered a stroke, and he now lives in the now. Alzheimer's victims live in the now. My cat Fergus. Maybe people once called lunatics.

I run marathons. I'm have diarrhea for days after the race.

I attend mindfulness classes. To help my marriage. The teacher is a Zen monk turned psychotherapist. He grew up in Pennsylvania and his golf handicap is three. We talk about Matthew McConaughey and *True Detective*.

I am manic depressive and alcoholic. I confuse admiration with affection.

That last from *Birdman*, directed by Alejandro Iñárritu, who also directed *21 Grams*, about a woman who loses both daughters to a traffic accident and a terminally ill mathematician whose wife does not love him. The title refers to the amount of weight a body loses at death.

Give up the ghost.

The cuckoo forlorn, paleontologists claim, evolved from a dinosaur.

Mental illness is stigmatized in Japan.

The blistered black skin on the first Godzilla resembles the burned flesh of Hiroshima and Nagasaki.

On March 1, 1954, the U.S. Military tested a hydrogen bomb near Bikini Atoll. The bomb was ten times more powerful than the one that devastated Hiroshima. One-hundred miles east of the blast, eighteen miles into the safe zone, sailed the Lucky Dragon No. 5, a Japanese tuna boat. Whitish ash snowed onto the deck. The crew vomited over the rails. Two weeks later, the ship reached Yaizu, its home port. The men were hospitalized in Tokyo. Six months later, the radio operator died. Japanese doctors concluded radiation sickness. The US government objected.

Eight months after the tragedy, *Godzilla* opens. Sailors lounge on the decks of a fishing boat. A harmonicist breathes a plaintive tune, and a guitarist accompanies, and those close move to the music. Others play board games, some just sit around and bullshit. A glare enormously up-bubbles not a knot from the prow. Tables overturn, scatter the dominoes, the guitar twangs. The ship is burning.

The toy ship. Godzilla destroys miniatures. When I was a boy, I watched the chintzy special effects on TV's Afternoon Express, hosted by Sonic Man. He introduced old monster flicks, wore a cape and goggles, and spoke his own language. "Amserx Poxies."

Eiji Tsubuyara created what Godzilla destroys. Before his Toho Studios fame, he served as assistant cameraman on *A Page of Madness*, an avant-garde film, lost for decades, of a mother confined in an asylum. The father is the janitor there. The daughter's arrival triggers tragic flashbacks.

Still barely married I consult in secret a divorce attorney. "How will my suicidal tendencies, revealed in memoirs, affect my custody suit?"

Seeing my daughter only half her life is self-murder enough. Say sentimental all you want, and you will, but she is it and nothing else for me to love, if love means terror of loss and of found-ness.

To raise the $200 for the consult, I accumulated stray cash in the pages of *Hitchcock / Truffaut*. I scheduled a day to divorce. But it snowed, and my daughter's crisp ecstasy erased my resolve.

I have begun a new fund in Geoff Dyer's *Zona*.

Have you seen *A Woman in the Dunes*? The black-and-white can't blanche the woman, the night-sand falls, glosses her naked skin golden. The insect-hunter she entraps remains when freedom's ladder lowers. Her daughter and husband are buried in the sand. Only houses with men garner rations. Cigarettes and sake.

Godzilla thunders through Tokyo, as uncaring of high-rises as we, on the beach, are of the grit. We desire the far pier, where the arcade is. Where is Godzilla bent? The tanks and planes fire on his (or is it her?) back. He stops. It is night. He turns his head toward his attackers. No one has witnessed this. He arches his back, gapes wide his titanic jaws, and he roars, fierce and pitiful, Promethean, Lear-hollow, *Howl* abundant. From his gullet gushes hydrogen enough for a hundred Hiroshimas. Tokyo melts like a toy.

Drag a resin-primed leather glove over a double bass whose strings are loose.

Never in your small art use the word "Holocaust."

Now you are not a monster.

ゴジラ

GODZILLA

You find your wife's profile on a singles site you just joined. Her best feature, you learn, is her back, and she prefers nonsmokers (you are a nonsmoker) but would tolerate those who do. You think, I will take up cigarettes and pull-ups. Then, Not until she posts a sexy picture. Finally, This comedy is Romantic or Black.

I didn't dupe her with a fake profile into a virtual affair. Though it would have been grist for my future divorce attorney.

Our daughter is thirteen. Because of her, I buried my suicide plan.

Rupert Holmes, who wrote The Pina Colada Song, lost his daughter to a brain tumor. She was ten. He recorded his hit, also called Escape, seven years before. A bored husband answers a personal seeking a man who likes the coconut cocktail. The seeker is his wife, equally bored. The song's Romcom conclusion: We have more in common than we thought, let's fuck in the cape's dunes. The drink tasted to Holmes like Kaopectate.

I vomit in the middle of the night. That's gross, people say. Instead of, You poor man.

I forwarded my wife an article on this condition. She said, What do you expect, being so depressed?

Other studies sent: men struggle to share emotion, men for well-being require regular sex, suicide more common in men.

It's sad, she observed, how you identify with what you lack.

After a lecture I delivered on melancholy a man with a crew-cut said, at birth God scoops a hole in our soul.

Bob Dylan recorded "My Bucket's Got a Hole In it." He looks into the sea and sees "the crabs and the fishes / doin' the be-bop-bee."

Rolling Stone compared the young Holmes to Dylan.

Hole, Courtney Love's band, covered Dylan's "It's All Over Now, Baby Blue."

If I knew my child would live with me half the time, I would divorce.

Wouldn't you fear loneliness? No, I would be the empty-handed painter drawing crazy patterns.

When does edgy, erratic verve turn unsexy? Before you say a word.

Words, words.

Hamlet claimed there is nothing outside of pompous Polonius that he would willingly part with, "except my life, except my life, except my life."

My last girlfriend before I got married believed Hamlet is punning. Accept.

Hamlet's jester Yorick, whose skull the Prince lifted, was full-on Keaton, knock-about-wise. Why else would the Prince, sick of pratfalls, turn fanatic for punning, the most virtual humor?

Gravity grounds Buster, but the pun hovers forever between this and that, that and this.

One afternoon in the White Cube Gallery, my daughter and I bonded over the death-head of Hirst, bejeweled as Jezebel.

My comedy, a pun, is Black: limbo between the child who holds me above dirt and the wife who harries me into it.

She has just posted a picture on the site. It is more maternal than erotic.

Smoke: you can't breathe it but it is still spirit.

I have massaged her back many times.

I always think, We will have fuck.

She, I have borne him a thousand times.

SHOCK

Our honeymoon in Avignon we woke to the crouching man. "Help you?" I rasped. You screamed, he vanished.

I was the one left the glass door open.

Cranach my new find, I say, while stirring the gin. You stare out the window at the mint. "Let your mom get you that print of *Melancholy*. She doesn't have to fucking live with you."

Tell that to Dana Andrews, who craves a painted woman & rolls into holes a small metal ball. He smokes two packs a day, bourbon before lunch. Older Andrews, graveled by his habits, works in UK pulp. *The Night of the Demon*. Getting through the séance: heroic.

Kate Bush conjures the demon in "Hounds of Love." Before I married you, her dreaming entranced me in a car. "I can't talk, I am in another world," I said.

Celtic honeymoons are of stone.

We thought an old house would keep us improving. I first hoist a sledge, I demo the hall. The lead I inhaled, not drinking, impairs my brain.

Our second home: rotting, too, but we own power tools.

Andrews nor anyone else saw Laura, Gene Tierney, in the sack. You study Gene, you don't think nipples. Couture.

Jayne Mansfield was the first to flash her breasts in mainstream cinema, '63, year Kennedy was killed.

Tierney fucked Jack. He dropped her for politics.

Tierney's daughter Daria, because of a fan's rubella, was born deaf and half-blind and mentally impaired. The actress herself, bipolar. Twenty-seven shock treatments.

For my moods, I swallow eight pills a day. If I walk into my state's asylum, I might never emerge again.

You would not stand outside the gate.

Would you tell our child I would hurt her?

There was that time in the night I thought your hair was a weasel. And when I told you I'd sheared my eyelashes.

Don't take her away.

We witnessed a portal. Had we stayed quiet, let the man through, how then would our little one cross alone.

FINIS
ELLA'S MEMO

You stuff a duffel, running shoes, lithium, whisky, a poem by our child on clocks and the moon. You fling the bag into the cab of your truck. You sit at the table. I enter. I am leaving you, you say. Do it this time, I reply. The poem creases. You empty your bag.

POLARIS'S ROOM
(MEMORANDUM)

I draw where blank spaces are.

I love when blanks appear on memos.

The memo announces this meeting. At the head of table, a man wears glasses. He says, Sine qua non.

I sit to his left.

He is not left-handed. If he were, with my left hand, I would write, Who is writing this question?, while with my right hand I would answer, The man who is writing this question.

I look at the memo. I take the pencil in my left hand. It is very sharp. I draw where the blank spaces are.

I was whimsical the day they sentenced me here. For the longest time, I was in my room making nothing happen. Then outside something I did. Those watching said, Who? Polaris? They said, Why both eyes?

I am filling the blank spaces with eyes. It is hard to stay on the page.

The skin on the bespectacled man is pale.

I love most when blankness appears on a face.

The left hand doesn't know what the right hand is doing.

The empty spaces I make where the man's eyes were.

On the inside of his head, I draw eyes of my own.

BOOK VI

Ella's husband stole her bowl. He hated how she chewed her food, thoroughly, until it turned liquid. She fled the small wooden house, and she reached the middle of a road.

Ella saw no car was going to kill her. The drivers were too skilled. They swerved away from her or stopped before they reached her.

Ella took to the forest.

She wandered without food or water for many days, imagining this would be an easier way to go.

She still was not dead when she looked at her hands. An eyeball was embedded in each palm. She found she could see out of these eyes. With them, she studied her face.

She was no longer a woman she knew.

She was something quite different.

Was this how death is?

Maybe the hunger and thirst had worked. She closed her palms and willed her attention to the eyes in her head. If this was the land of the dead, she wanted to look through her old eyes. She noticed nothing different. There were trees, and on the ground, brown leaves. Stones large and small were about.

Ella saw a stone the size of a head and remembered, I have a young daughter, and then she thought, I've got to go back.

The child had lost her bowl.

Ella had walked so long, she was lost. She looked at the

sky. The sky was gray.

She lowered her head, and there was a small wooden house.

Ella fled from the house into a road. She stood in the middle. Cars sped toward her. None touched her.

She rushed into the forest near the road. She walked. Hunger weakened her, and thirst.

She tripped over a head-sized stone. With her hands, she broke her fall.

There was pain in her hands. Her palms were gashed.

Ella studied the cuts. Inside each, she glimpsed white. She recalled bones and eyeballs. She imagined seeing her head from her hands.

The head she saw was not the one she remembered.

Pain was in her hands.

She imagined seeing her hands from her head. The gashes were red.

The head Ella had felt bigger than the stone she stumbled over.

She had a young daughter, a child, and the child had nothing to eat.

Ella would save her.

How to reach her?

A house appeared, small and wooden.

Through a window Ella saw a man. He was holding a spoon before the face of a girl.

Ella rushed onto the porch. She grabbed the door knob. The metal scalded her hand. She jerked it away. She stared at the palm. The shape of a spoon's oval bowl reddened its center. Pain was there.

Ella touched the shape to her lips.

Pain. Tongue, teeth, throat.

Ella imagined living inside of the pain, seeing the world from there.

She saw three people before an oven, a man to the left, and a woman to the right, and in the middle, a small girl, who was holding the hand of the man and the hand of the woman. The girl was looking up at the man. The man was plump. The woman was gaunt.

Ella was seeing from the pain. She was starving. She was falling down. A small hand was holding the hand not burned. The hand slipped away and she fell.

From the leafy ground, she saw near her head the head of a woman. Where the woman's eyes once were, was blood.

Ella could drink the blood. She had no bowl.

She struggled to raise herself and flee to this vessel.

BOOK VII

Otto had not noticed his wife for three days when he recalled she had wandered out into the ice.

He was cold. He was sitting where the mirrors are. He looked for his face in the mirrors but saw only a dark gray oval surrounded by lighter gray. When he moved his head, the oval moved, so the oval, he concluded, must be of his making.

But how changed he was. The last time he had noticed his wife, three days ago, Otto had looked into the mirrors and seen, yes, an oval, but the oval was white, with two black holes where the eyes should be, a black line where the mouth should be, and a faint upside down triangle between the eyes and mouth, suggesting a nose.

That day—three days ago, was it?—yes, that day three days ago Otto had awakened with his wife beside him. The room had been cold, but not so cold you couldn't move. Otto had looked at his wife. Like him, she possessed an oval head. It was pale, and its eyes were dark, and so was its mouth, and its nose was a vague triangle, upside down.

The difference between his head and hers, though, was that she, being a woman, had long hair. The hair was black, as his shorter hair was.

When Otto had first met his wife, a very long time ago, neither of them looked like they had looked three days ago. During that time, so long ago Otto could not remember how long, they both had faces with tanned-pinkish cheeks, eyes white with blue dots in their centers, and well-defined noses, through which they, Otto and his wife, breathed, effortlessly, for the air around them was mild. Both husband and wife at that time enjoyed color in their hair. Otto's was short and golden. His wife's was longer, and it was auburn.

I have never seen you in a dream, Otto said on that day they met so long ago. That must mean that you are real.

Maybe, she replied, but what matters is I am here.

She was standing under an oak tree whose branches had not yet fallen under the weight of ice. The tree was not even dead. It stood in a wide green field.

Otto had seen her from far away. His eyes were strong then. He reached her quickly, and was by her side when he said his first words to her, about how she had not appeared in his dreams.

What the two of them had done between that day a long time ago, too long to remember how long, and the day only three days ago when Otto's wife last awakened beside him: this was not difficult to recall. The two of them walked through the world, large and alive. They walked through fields, forests, mountains, even deserts. They walked holding hands. But they were looking away.

Why did they look away? This question arose in Otto's head when he was recalling that his wife had wandered out alone into the ice, when he was cold and where the mirrors are and gazing at the image he was making, a gray oval surrounded with lighter gray.

They looked away, not from the grass or trees or sand, but from each other. They did this because staring too hard into bright eyes set in a tan-pinkish face is terrifying.

Look into alert eyes, and you see reflected your own face, also alert. But this face is no longer your face. It does not exist as the flesh hiding your skull. Your face belongs to the face at which you stare. It lives inside of the skull behind the face at which you stare.

You are a prisoner inside this skull. You lie on its floor of bone until you are forced by the pulpy orb above to move. You are forced to breathe, to walk, to glare at yourself in mirrors, the mirrors all around you, mirrors of polished bone. You are surrounded by the face that once belonged to you, and always appearing beside this face, is her face, and it looks exactly like your old face. And when you turn to the side and expect to see her, you see nothing but white, the bone-white walls. She is not there. Only you are there. Then you look into the mirror again, and there, beside your old face, is her face, the same as your old face. You turn again, expect to see her, but there is white.

This was why, Otto said to himself as he was recalling that his wife had wandered out in the ice three days earlier, this was why he and his wife, back before there was ice, did not look at each other as they traveled hand-in-hand over the grass and under the trees and over the sands.

They knew the terror that existed in each other's eyes, in each other's skulls, for just as sure as Otto was no longer himself but shrunken into a prison in his wife's skull, so she was no longer herself, but diminished to an inmate inside of his head. He could feel her breathing and walking in there, and then standing still and staring, and seeing her old face in the polished walls, and also a face resembling it exactly, only the face was his.

Otto first became the creature in her skull, and she in his, on the day they had first met, there in the green field under the oak tree. Just after he had told her that he had never seen her in a dream, and so she must be real, and just after she had told him that all that mattered was that she was there, they had looked into each other's eyes.

This was the first time. It was also the last time.

But after all, Otto thought as he began to guess how far into the ice his wife had wandered, this is what marriage is.

By the time Otto had last awakened beside his wife, three days ago now, or so he believed, he and his wife had almost perfected their marriage. They had done this by looking away from each other's eyes for so long, that that they were growing into forms other than the diminished ones in each other's skulls, the ones with tanned-pinkish faces and bright eyes.

Three days ago, Otto and his wife had become white faces with black holes where their eyes should be, and black lines where their mouths once were, and vague upside down triangles in the places of their noses.

Otto knew this because they had looked into the mirror together, and they looked exactly the same, save for his wife's longer black hair, of course, although, now that Otto thought of it, on that day, that day three days ago, the length of his wife's hair might have been the same as his own.

Regardless of how much they resembled each other, however, Otto and his wife were obviously no longer the same shrunken beings living in each other's skulls. And there were not trapped in walls of polished bone. They were dwelling in ice.

Otto knew this because he was cold, cold all the time, and

all around him was a white entirely flat, quite different from the grayish white of bone.

Otto now felt colder than ever, sitting alone in the ice and looking into the mirrors and seeing only a gray oval surrounded by lighter gray.

His wife was not there. She had gone wandering into the ice some time ago. Oh yes, three days ago. Why had she gone walking out onto the ice?

Otto was cold, the coldest he had ever been. His eyes were freezing. He closed them. On the inside of his left lid he saw the oak tree under which he had first looked into the eyes of his wife. She was not under the tree. He was not, either.

There was the tree. It was not dead, nor was the grass surrounding it dead. The tree had the look of a tree that had never not been there, and also of a tree that had never shaded two people, a man and woman. No one had ever been near this tree. This tree was far and solitary.

Otto felt feeling leave his feet and his hands. His head felt lighter. Something that was in his head was no longer in his head. Fog filled the empty space. The fog was cold.

Otto knew enough to know he needed warmth. But he couldn't remember how he had found warmth before. Whatever had leaked out of his head, had taken memories with it. He looked for memories still in his head.

Yes. Here was one. It was hidden in fog and cold, but it was there.

Once something was beside him. He was lying down, and a breathing thing was touching him. The breathing was the heat. He could not remember how this thing, no, it was a person, yes, a person, he could not remember how this person looked, what it, wait, it was a woman. What was this woman doing beside him? She resembled how he thought he now looked. There was pain in her face. Otto felt the pain in his head. The pain was, yes, he remembered, the pain was his wife. The pain was hot in his head. It was fire.

But Otto felt that his legs and arms could no longer feel. The fire was gone. Cold fog filled where it was.

Whatever was left in his head whispered to him, he must find warmth.

He could wander out into the ice. The woman—who?—the woman, she might be out on the ice. She would warm him, there would be the pain of numbness withdrawing, she would tell him who she was.

Otto needed to open in his eyes. He needed to walk.

Hadn't something just appeared on his left eyelid? What? Only black was now there.

Otto tried to open his eyes. They were frozen shut. He tried harder. The right lid opened, and then the left.

In front of him was a mirror. He saw a whitish oval, featureless, smooth. It did not move.

The moistness on both eyes froze solid. The ghostly oval vanished.

Otto saw only the ice covering his eyes. It was thick and white. He could not close his eyes. He could not move them.

Otto felt all feeling leave his torso, his chest, his face.

His frozen body was heavy, but his head was light. All that once was in it was gone. Foggy cold floated through the emptiness.

One being remained in his head, amidst the fog, a frozen man rising from a frozen earth, a figure of white, statue more than man, which could not look nor be looked upon.

This was what Otto last saw, for now he felt the loss of the self that was seeing the white.

Where Otto was not, white was.

But something remained in the spreading ice that was not ice: a craving for what was not there, a warmth, a woman, an oak, anything, could be anything, and so this craving was terrible in its freedom, and, beyond consummation, terrible in its pain.

POLARIS'S ROOM
(PURSUIT)

The car is not black. Paranoiacs fear black.

The car is blue, dark blue, so dark it nearly is not blue. This blue is not in the world, in the sky or a flower.

The car is there. Polaris is called a fugitive.

A fugitive is pursued. A true pursuer pursues but does not apprehend. If she apprehends, she will no longer be a pursuer. Who will she then be?

The truest pursuer is female. Women are desperate for affection. Fugitives are lonely and criminal.

It is not the blue that is unique. It is the desperation.

I found myself inside a house. There was a woman. She was staring at me. I was staring at her. Behind her face, a person was hiding.

I recognized this person. This person had been watching me. It had been watching me when I could not watch it back, when I was looking down or in a basement or watching someone sleep.

I peeled away the woman within whom the person was hiding. The person was a woman. Her eyes were unworldly blue, and they were desperate.

I fled.

The woman shadows me. She is in the car.

She steals into other women when I am not watching, and

she watches me.
    I find these women.
    I skin them, and there she is, desperate and blue, and I flee.
    Black is for the paranoid.
    My terror is of only blue.

ELLA'S MEMO

Your glasses I hid under the pillow. After the first time. There was a mountain. And you admired a woman carried her own condoms. The next day, movie, *The Fisher King*. Crazed poet, murdered wife. I feared your own mania. But you confessed when you were seven Johnny sat naked on the linoleum and played with sock-dolls and you stayed clothed. Next we lived on the highway, nighttime trucks rattle the windows, sewage rises into the tub, and during a blizzard you tell me about the trucker who dangled his left arm out his rig's window and by the time he reached Salinas, gangrene. The city now. You pass the big exam, I rue how long since I was properly fucked. I vanish into the avenue. Lost, I am hard as bone, and found.

BOOK VIII

The husband awoke once more to find a boar at the foot of his bed. Like before, he screamed. The scream, like always, awakened his wife, and she screamed, too, not at the boar, which she did not see, but at her husband's screaming, which terrified her every time. She shouted, "It's another of your night terrors. Go back to sleep!"

The husband felt very bad for waking up his wife almost every night. But he couldn't help what happened to him in his sleep, could he? The boar always looked the same. It was not quite as big as a grown black bear, nor was it as small as a bloodhound. It was always standing, with its snout tilted slightly down. Its tusks were curved and long and sharp, like the tusks of a real boar might be. The beast did not look fierce, however. Its eyes, or what the husband could see of its eyes in the dark, resembled the eyes of a stuffed animal, the kind the husband's daughter might have played with, if she were his daughter. The husband would have said the eyes were sad.

But this beast, sad or not, was harming the husband's marriage. His wife no longer wanted to sleep with him. However, since the only other bedroom in the house was occupied, and since the couch in the parlor was uncomfortable, she continued to sleep in the same bed with him.

And it's not as if the husband saw the boar at the foot of his bed *every* night. Sometimes he would go weeks without seeing the boar, or anything else—he sometimes saw other figures in his room at night—and so his wife would believe that his night terror days were over. During these periods, she and the husband would sleep through the night and wake up each morning feeling happy and ready for whatever thing the day might bring, no matter how awful.

But now almost every night the husband saw the boar. He and his wife crawled out of bed in the morning with aching eyes and heads, and feared that every moment throughout the day might bring the worst thing possible.

The wife said to him at the end of one of these days, "I have put up with your night terrors long enough. If you don't seek help for them, I can no longer live with you."

The husband couldn't think of anything to say in reply, so he nodded.

The next day, after another terrible night, the husband went to a doctor. The doctor asked, "What seems to be the problem?"

The husband told him. The doctor asked, "Has something upsetting happened to you?"

The husband thought for a minute and then said, yes, something very bad happened a few years ago.

"What?" asked the doctor.

The husband looked at the floor. Then he said, well, no, nothing really that bad, I don't think, nothing worth mentioning at least.

The doctor said, "I need to know everything about you so that I can help you."

The husband looked at the floor. It was black. He told the doctor about this job he once had but had lost it and how that made him sad.

The doctor concluded, "It is this sad thing disturbing your nights. You need to see another doctor. This is his name."

That night before bed, the wife asked, "Well, what did the doctor say?" The husband told her, and she said, "Go see that other doctor tomorrow. I am dying here. Can't you see that?"

That night the husband once more saw the boar at the foot of its bed. Again he was going to scream before he could become aware of exactly what was happening, but then he remembered something for just a second and then this something passed but the pause reminded him that he should not scream. This had not happened before. The husband clamped his jaws shut. What came out was a grunt.

Just as his wife sprung awake, the husband thought he saw the boar, for the first time, step toward him. Before he could be sure, his wife screamed. Then she said to him, as she always did, "You've had another night terror. Go back to sleep!" She added, "And go see that doctor tomorrow!"

The husband and his wife woke with aching eyes and heads and shuffled through the day expecting the worst.

The husband did go to the other doctor that day. This second doctor was much like the last, except he didn't take the husband's weight or pulse. He didn't even touch the husband. He asked him about his night visions. The husband told him. Then the second doctor asked, "What about this job you lost?"

The husband could not quite remember the job he had told the first doctor he had lost. But he did not say this, because didn't want anyone to think he was crazy. He was vague. He said, yes, he had lost a job some time ago and this had made him sad.

"What was the job?" asked the second doctor.

The husband looked at the floor. It was bright white. It hurt the husband's eyes. He closed them. He thought of the job. He tried to recall the job. Then he remembered something but forgot it again, and he opened his eyes and the floor seemed even brighter so he looked away as he told the second doctor that his job was to take care of something.

"What did you take care of?" the second doctor asked.

Something very valuable, the husband said.

"Be more specific," the second doctor said.

Very, very valuable, the husband said. Precious.

"Was it alive or dead?" asked the second doctor.

Most definitely alive, the husband said. As he did, he had to look up at the ceiling, so bright was the floor.

"That is all the time we have," the second doctor said. "You should see my colleague. Here is his name. He can help you more than I can. Meanwhile, here is some medicine. Take it tonight before you go to bed."

The husband told his wife about what had happened at the second doctor's. She said, "Go see that other doctor tomorrow. Take a double dose of medicine. I'm dying to get some sleep."

The husband took a single dose. This time when he woke up in the middle of the night, it was different. He was still in his bed, but the bed was not in his room. It was somewhere where it was green, very dark green, like a forest you heard about when you were a child, a forest where people you would never see made strange objects with sticks, rocks, and hair. They would leave these strange objects just beside the paths. If you were curious and followed them, you might never come back.

89

Where was the boar? It was not at the foot of his bed. At the foot of his bed was something brown. It was the size of a head. He reached for it. It was not a head. It was a piece of meat. The husband was very hungry, so he grabbed the meat. It was moist and warm, and it smelled like the forest you heard of as a child. The husband bit into the meat.

It was not cooked very well. It was not even cooked at all. It tasted like rusted iron. Juice ran down his chin. The husband felt sick, but he wanted to eat more. He bit again. He felt sicker, but he chewed ferociously.

Then the husband vomited. He groaned while he was vomiting, like he had been gored in the belly.

He heard his wife scream. He was not in the forest any longer. He was not eating meat shaped like a head but not a head. He was still in his bed, though. His wife was near him. He felt her hair on his face. Her neck was near his mouth. He tasted salt on his lips. This salt was from her neck, which sweated when she slept.

"Get off me! What are you doing? What are you doing? Are you trying to kill me?"

She pushed him away. She was breathing hard and angrier than he had ever seen her before. She told him that he had awakened her by biting her neck. She told him to get the hell out of that bed and not get back into it until he had seen the third doctor. He asked her, where should he sleep? She said she didn't care, just not in this bed.

The husband shuffled out of the bedroom carrying his pillow and a blanket. The door slowly closed behind him. It almost clicked closed but did not. He stood in the hall. Where should he sleep? The other bedroom door was closed, as usual. The room was, as he well knew, occupied. He had not been in there in a long time. He did not want to disturb anything. He was also afraid of what might happen.

He lay on the stiff couch. He nodded off only near the dawn.

He was awakened by something moving upstairs. It was not his wife. She did not make sounds like that.

He was out the door before she came down.

The third doctor looked like the second doctor, except the third doctor had a beard. He asked the husband if the medicine had worked. The husband said he didn't know, he wasn't quite sure what it was supposed to do. The third doctor told him not to worry, that what was bothering him couldn't be fixed by medicine anyway. What could fix him was understanding why he was seeing what he was seeing. Why was he seeing a boar and not something else?

"Think," the third doctor said, "of something in your childhood that had to do with an animal. A big animal. A dog maybe, or even an actual pig."

The husband said that when he was a child, he did not play with animals. He played with dolls. He had several dolls of little blond-haired, blue-eyed children. They were not small dolls, the husband said, but big dolls, almost as big as those dummies ventriloquists use. They were life-like, the husband said, and they were also made long ago. One of his grandparents had given them to him.

The third doctor nodded his head as if he understood something. Then he said, "What memories do you have of playing with these children?"

The husband stared at the floor. He had never seen a floor

like this. It looked like it was made of glass, though he could not see anything on the other side of it, nor could he exactly see his own reflection in it. He saw blurry shapes in it. They were moving.

The husband could not answer this question. He was too mesmerized by the floor. He asked the third doctor what this floor was made of. The doctor said that he did not know. The doctor asked again about the memories and the children.

The husband continued to look at the floor. Then something came to him. He said he remembered one day he was playing near the woods with these dolls. He was pretending that they were a family, a father and a mother and a daughter. When he came in for supper that night, he noticed that the doll that was the daughter had disappeared. He ran back to the edge of the wood, but the doll was gone. He knew his parents would be angry with him for losing the doll. The doll was also his favorite. He stared into the woods. It was getting dark, and so he could see very little. He wondered if the doll had somehow made it into the woods. He was forbidden to go into the woods himself. He had to recover the doll, though.

He entered the woods. All light was gone. He heard a sound. It was like an animal, a big animal. He felt as if this animal were looking at him. He was afraid but he also loved the doll and he needed to find the doll. And so he pushed further into the dark wood.

He heard the sound again. It was a grunting sound. He saw a huge figure in his path. The creature was on all fours. He saw its eyes. They were blue. Under the eyes were two giant tusks. This was a boar. Its head was tilted toward the ground. It made the sound again. This sound was not a grunting sound. It was a whimpering sound. This boar was sick.

The husband as a boy was no longer afraid. The boar needed help. He stepped toward the boar, and he saw that in the boar's mouth was his doll. The boy reached for the doll. The boar opened its mouth, and the doll fell out and hit the ground. The boy reached down to pick the doll up.

Then the boy found himself back at his house in his bed. He was still half-asleep. He felt very dizzy and weak and hot. He could not get awake. He kept drifting back into sleep. When he fell into these fitful sleeps, he dreamed of being in a cave where boars had been. He smelled their earthy animal smell and he smelled blood and he smelled rotting flesh. When he struggled awake from these sleeps, he could not get this feeling of being in a boar cave out of his head. Was he in a boar cave or in his room?

What told him he was in his room was what he saw at the foot of his bed. It was the size of a small child. He sat up and grabbed it. It was the doll, the daughter doll. He held it close. It was solid and smelled of earth. He said to himself, this is real.

The husband stopped speaking, and looked up from the glassy floor in the third doctor's office. The third doctor was staring at him. He said, "That explains it all, don't you see? This boar you are seeing at night is simply a projection of a childhood fear. You are afraid of abandonment. You saw your doll as a companion to keep you from feeling lonely. You associate this animal you saw as a child with the things that take away what you love. The question is, why is this animal, this projection, appearing to you now with such frequency. Have you suffered a recent loss that might have recalled all of these repressed childhood feelings?"

The husband looked at the floor again. He said that he had lost a job. When the third doctor asked him what kind of job, the husband said that his job was to take care of something. Then the doctor asked what he cared for. The husband said that he took care of something extremely valuable. The doctor asked what it was. The husband looked up, closed his eyes, shook his head from side to side, and said, "Something alive."

"We are out of time," said the third doctor. "Here is your task until we meet again. Remember that the boar is nothing but a projection of your fear of abandonment. If you can overcome this fear, the boar will vanish."

The husband lay in the bed with his wife later that night. He told her what had happened with the third doctor. His wife asked him how he felt. The husband asked her why she asked. She told him that he looked very sad, sadder than she had ever seen him before, and then she added, now that's saying something, since you, my dear, have been one sad man, for as long as I have known you. And then she gave him a hug and said that she believed that all would be right now, that his terrors were over and now they would rest. The husband wanted to cry just at that moment, but he did not.

This time the husband woke up in the middle of the night and did not see a boar at the foot of his bed. He and his wife and a little girl with blond hair and blue eyes were in the woods. The woods were sunny. This little girl was probably ten-years-old. She was beautiful. She sat between the husband and the wife. There was a big fire burning in front of them. Behind them was a white tent, a perfect size for three. The little girl reached out and held the husband's hand. She looked at him and smiled. The husband smiled back.

This girl was his child. She was his wife's child. They were a family. They were camping in the woods. His wife said they would need more wood for the fire, and would he and his lovely little girl like to go fetch some.

The husband and his child had wandered from camp. They needed to find more wood for the fire. It was getting dark and cold.

"Daddy," the child said, "are there any wild animals in this part of the forest?"

"No, child," the husband said. "This part of the forest is safe. I used to play here as a child. I would bring my favorite doll out here and play. There was no danger at all."

"It is getting very dark. Shouldn't we head back?"

"We need more wood, dear child. We will turn back soon."

"But I'm scared, daddy, and cold. Can we please go back?"

"Just a little while longer, my love."

"But I thought I heard something, like an animal. It was grunting."

"I'm sure you just heard your daddy clearing his throat. Look, just up that hill. A pile of wood! Like someone put it there for us. Let's fetch it. But wait. The hill is steep, and you are tired. You stay here and rest. Sit on this stump, and I will run up the hill and grab the wood. You can watch me the whole time. I won't go out of your sight. I will return faster than you can say Jack Robinson."

The child said, "Jack Robinson," and then, "Too late," and laughed. The husband laughed, too.

He leapt up the hill, grabbed the wood quickly, and turned to descend.

The stump was empty. He dropped the wood, stumbled

down the hill. The child was gone. He called for her. Nothing. He called again, louder, and again, nothing. He screamed her name as loudly as he could.

The husband woke up again, this time in his bed and in his bedroom, but he was not screaming. He was watching a man scream. The man was staring right at him and screaming. A woman lying beside the man jerked up and screamed, too.

The husband wanted to comfort the two screaming people, to tell them that there was nothing to fear, that what they thought they had lost was not really lost but alive and safe. But the man could not speak. When he tried only a grunt came out. This was how it had always been, a grunt, followed by a bowing of his head and an effort to heave all of what he wanted to say, but could not say, into his eyes. He wanted the man to see his eyes and know that nothing was lost, but only distant. What the man wanted, what the man was screaming for, was simply far, far away, too far for him to reach. But not lost.

The husband turned away from the man and the woman. They were still screaming. The husband hopped off the bed. He landed on all fours, lightly for a creature as large as he was. Then he did as he always did. He walked out of the door and into the hall and down the hall and toward the other bedroom, whose door was, as usual, closed. He walked through the door and into the room. The room was empty save for a rectangle of silvery glass, a rectangle as wide and tall as a child. This silvery glass was in the back corner. The creature walked through the glass. On the other side of the glass was a forest.

The creature moved through the forest easily, as he had so many mornings. He was returning to the cave at the bottom of the hill. When he got close, he heard the crying.

He reached the cave. The child was sitting on the ground at the cave's mouth. She had long blond hair and was wearing a white dress. It was very dirty, and it was tattered around the edges. The creature stood in front of her, three feet away.

The child stopped crying and stared at him. Her eyes were blue. Once more, she said, "Will you take me home to my mommy and daddy today?"

The creature wanted to say that he wished he could do this but he could not do this. He also wanted to say that though he wished he could take her home, he was also glad she was here, even though she was sad. He wanted to tell her that he loved her, that he had only wanted to be with her for a few hours on that day so long ago, when she and her father were gathering wood. He did not mean for her to remain lost.

Now it was too late. He threw all of his sorrow and love into his eyes and stared at the girl. Maybe this time, unlike all the mornings before, she would understand.

She looked down and began to cry. The creature closed his eyes, and he released his love and sorrow into his throat, and he squealed so loudly the girl put her hands to her ears. If someone other than the child had been there to hear the squealing, that man would have thought that a boar somewhere was awakening to a pain so terrible that it was almost a human pain.

POLARIS'S ROOM
(WEEKEND)

Leap alone from a quickening car.
I am crazy, you scream, enough.
As if someone would die with you.
Talk of the woman fired you up.
Flirtation to me as, to you, coitus.
Once you doubt once, everything is your terror.
A medium receives gust as ghost, you witness the abyss in my japes.
Which is why I Polaris the driver seize your arm before your door unlatches, and pin your hand to the wheel, and pull my own handle, and into the opening, no one.

POSTSCRIPT

Nicholas of Lynn sailed north, toward the hole at the pole.
1360. He saw pyramids of ice, they were churning. Nicholas
crossed into the current. Round and round and round. He
forgot his name. He fell asleep. At the vortex rose an obelisk.
Black. Nicholas knew this would happen. That was why he
came. Now he is in a book. The pages are white like ice.

> — Robert Henri, author of *The Art Spirit*,
> which influenced David Lynch, whose films
> reveal us riven, and of healing, terrified

About the author

Eric G. Wilson is author of *Against Happiness, Keep It Fake, Everyone Loves a Good Train Wreck, How to Make a Soul, The Mercy of Eternity, My Business Is to Create: Blake's Infinite Writing,* and other titles. His work has appeared in *The Virginia Quarterly Review, The Georgia Review, The Portland Review, The Oxford American, The Notre Dame Review, Hotel Amerika, Prelude, The Collagist, The Fanzine, Café Irreal, The Los Angeles Times, The New York Times, The Vestal Review,* and elsewhere. A recipient of a National Humanities Fellowship, he teaches Romanticism and creative writing at Wake Forest University.

CPSIA information can be obtained
at www.ICGtesting.com
Printed in the USA
BVOW09s1039230218
508899BV00001B/3/P